Mel Bay's

Children's Guitar Method

By William Bay

2

THE FULL G CHORD*

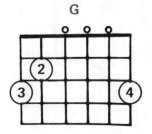

G

To play the full G chord - make certain that your left hand thumb is placed in the middle of the back of the neck. Bring your fingers directly down on the strings. Practice to make sure your fingers aren't touching and deadening the wrong strings.

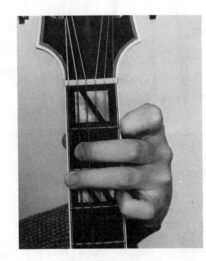

G

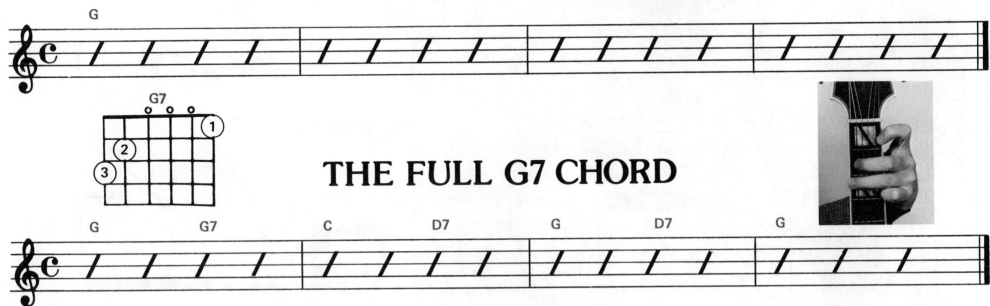

THE FULL G7 CHORD

G7

G   G7   C   D7   G   D7   G

*TEACHER'S NOTE - If the student's hand size is still too small to play the full G and G7 chord, continue with EZ form.

SHE'LL BE COMING ROUND THE MOUNTAIN

Sing & Play

AWAY IN A MANGER

THIS LITTLE LIGHT OF MINE

NOTE REVIEW

Teacher Accomp.:

MARCHING ALONG

SHORT PIECE

GUITAR BOOGIE

THE PLAYFUL PUPPY

THE NOTES ON THE FOURTH STRING (D)

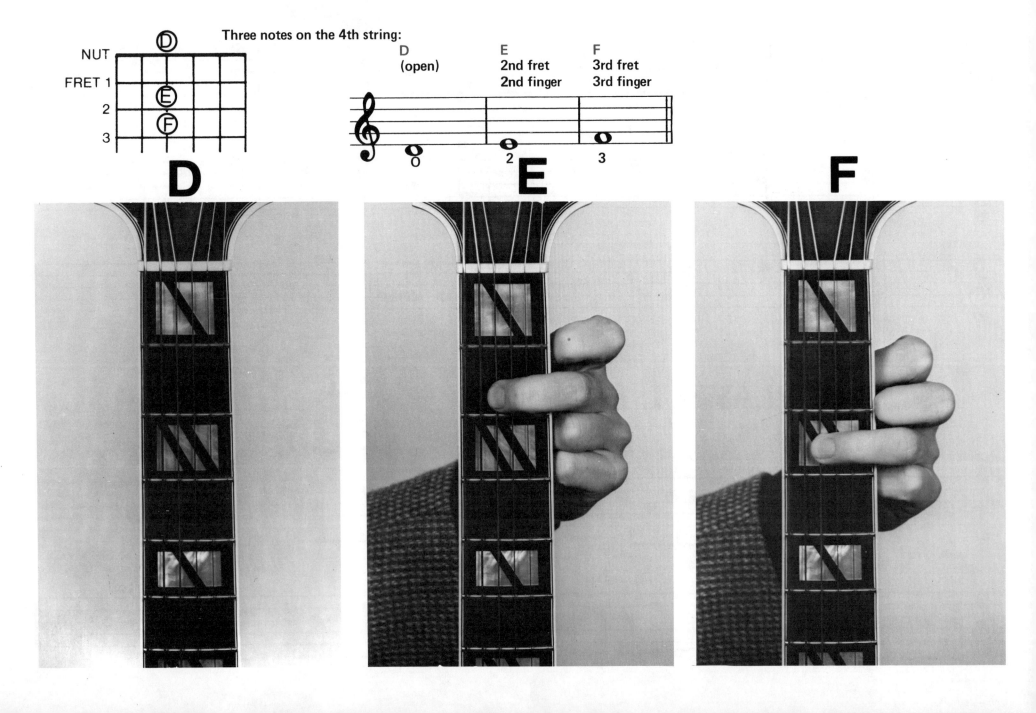

MYSTERY SOUNDS

MINOR MELODY

NOTE REVIEW

COUNT AND PLAY

REST SONG

AMAZING GRACE SOLO

Chords are for teacher accompaniment

HYMN

BUCKING BRONCO

OLD McDONALD'S FARM

DOTS BEFORE AND AFTER A DOUBLE BAR MEAN REPEAT THE MEASURES BETWEEN.

REPEAT SONG

DOTTED QUARTER NOTE

A Dotted Quarter Note looks like this ♩. . It is counted ♩. 1&2

Compare

STAND UP – SIT DOWN

DOTTED QUARTER NOTE

Count: 1 & 2 & 3 & 4 &

SOURWOOD MOUNTAIN

Teacher Accomp:

DOTTED QUARTER NOTE

Count: 1 & 2 & (etc.)

THE YELLOW ROSE OF TEXAS

(Chords are for teacher accompaniment)

ALL THROUGH THE NIGHT

(Chords are for teacher accompaniment)

TWO NEW CHORDS
D

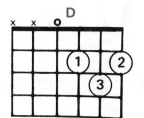

PLAY ONLY THE TOP 4 STRINGS

A7

PLAY ONLY THE TOP 5 STRINGS

BILLY BOY
(Sing and Strum)

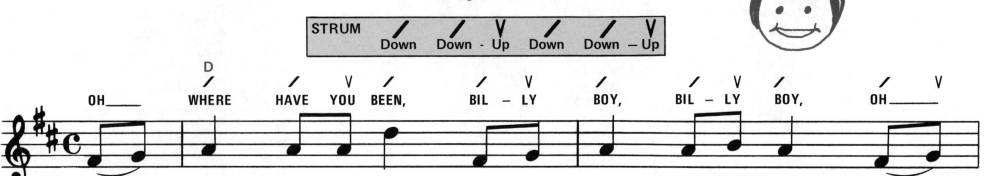

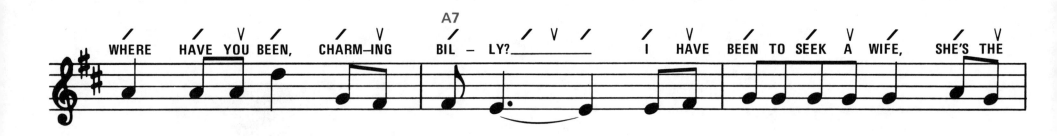

2. Can she bake a cherry pie? Billy boy, Billy boy,
   Can she bake a cherry pie? charming Billy.
   She can bake a cherry pie, quick's a cat can wink its eye,
   She's a young thing and cannot leave her mother.

CAMPTOWN RACES

(Sing and Strum)

PRAISE HIM ALL YE LITTLE CHILDREN

(Sing and Strum)

2. Love Him

3. Thank Him

JIMMY CRACK CORN
(Sing and Strum)

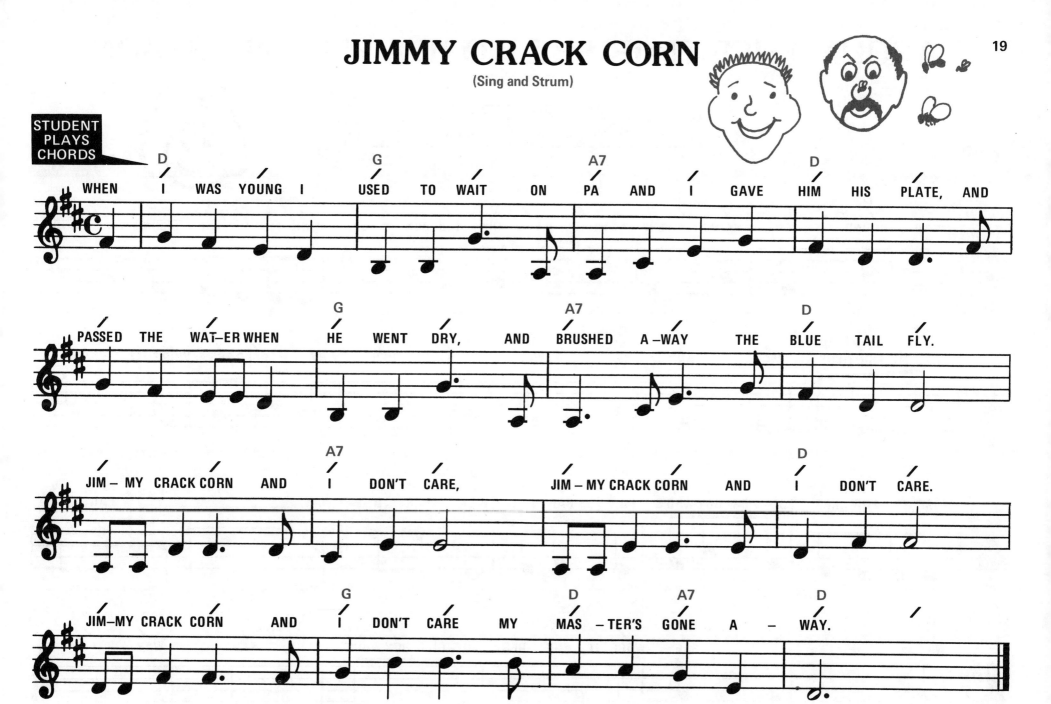

AROUND HER HAIR SHE WORE A YELLOW RIBBON

(Sing and Strum)

NOTES ON THE FIFTH STRING (A)

Three notes on the 5th string:

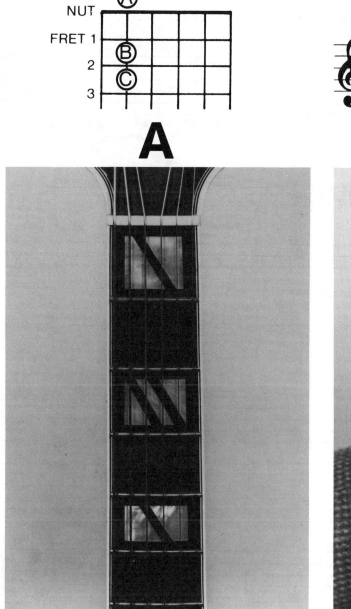

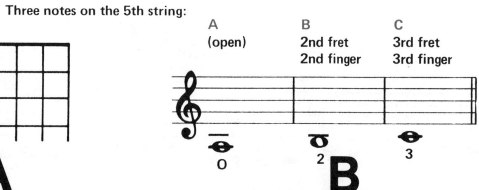

A	B	C
(open)	2nd fret	3rd fret
	2nd finger	3rd finger

A

B

C

I PLAY A

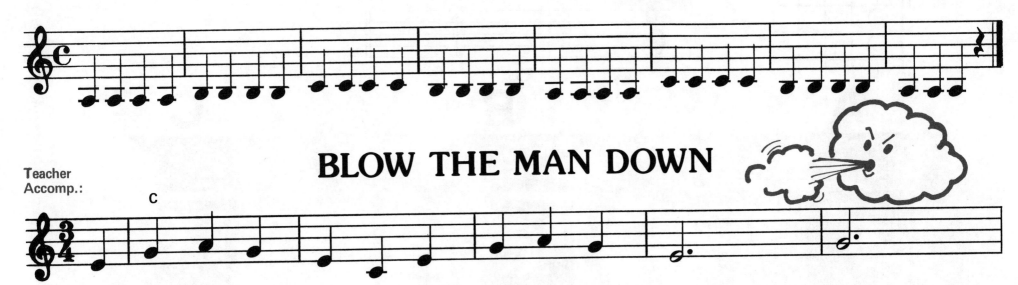

BLOW THE MAN DOWN

Teacher Accomp.:

OLD SMOKEY

CHINESE CHECKERS

RUNNING UP THE STRINGS

DOTTED QUARTER NOTE REVIEW

KUM-BA-YA

AFRICAN HYMN

MICHAEL, ROW THE BOAT ASHORE

SPIRITUAL

FRANKIE AND JOHNNY

THE CLOCK
(DUET)

Student plays TOP PART 1st time through — BOTTOM PART 2nd time through

THE RIDDLE SONG

SWEET BETSY FROM PIKE

THE C SCALE

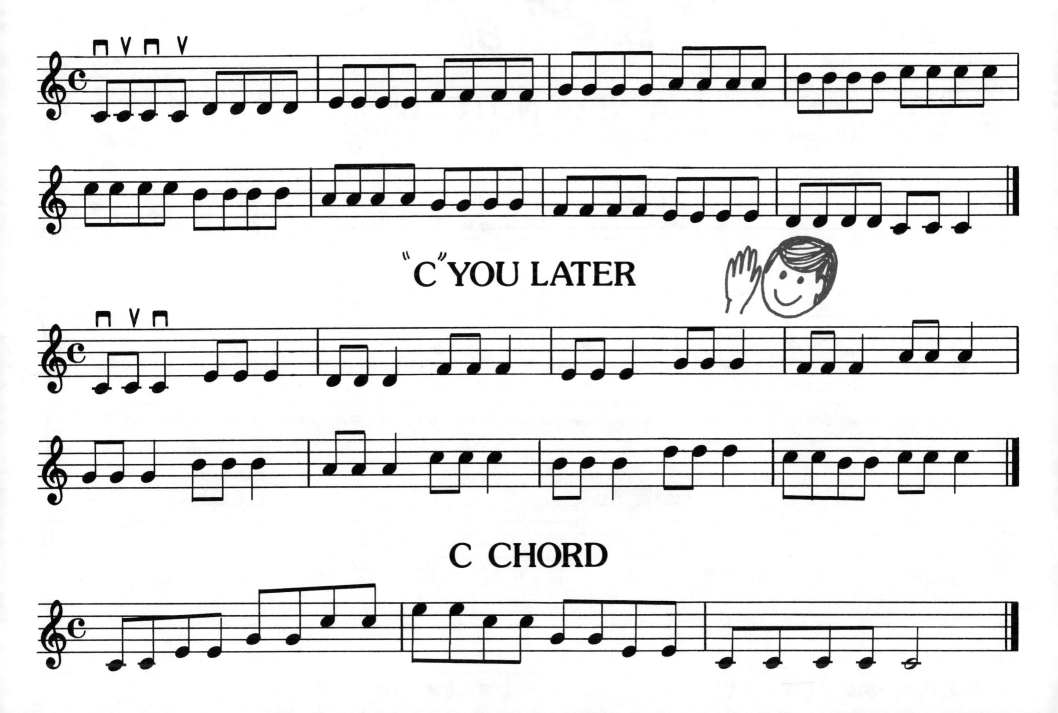

"C" YOU LATER

C CHORD

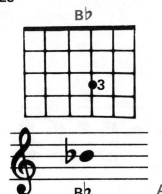

Bb

A NEW NOTE - B♭

A flat looks like this (♭). When a flat appears before a note, the note is lowered 1 fret.

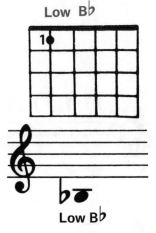

Low B♭

Low B♭

When a flat appears before a note, all similar notes in that measure will stay flatted unless a NATURAL Sign (♮) appears to cancel out the Flat.

STILL FLATTED

NATURAL SIGN CANCELS FLAT

OLD JOE CLARK

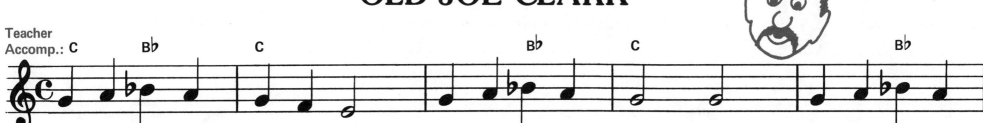

MARY ANN

29

KEY SIGNATURE

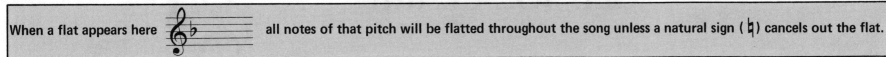

When a flat appears here all notes of that pitch will be flatted throughout the song unless a natural sign (♮) cancels out the flat.

TELL ME WHY

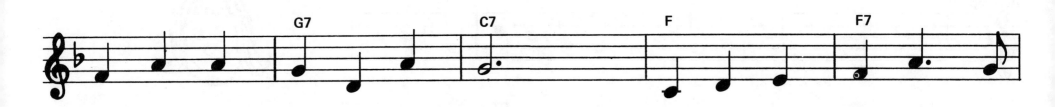

O COME ALL YE FAITHFUL

(Watch for the B♭ 's)

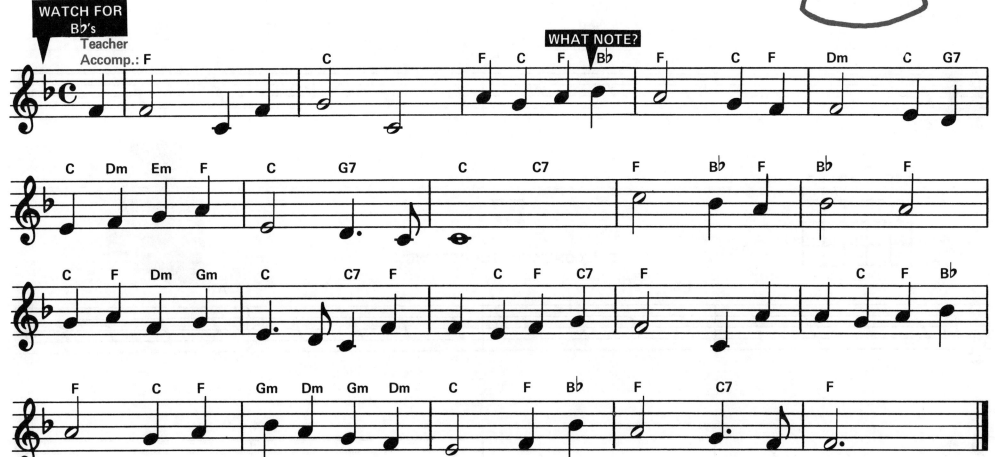

TWO NEW CHORDS
A

PLAY ONLY THE TOP 5 STRINGS

E7

PLAY ONLY THE TOP 6 STRINGS

MY BONNIE LIES OVER THE OCEAN

(Sing and Strum)

SILENT NIGHT
(Sing and Strum)

SI — LENT NIGHT, HO — LY NIGHT! ALL IS CALM

ALL IS BRIGHT, ROUND YOU VIR — GIN MOTH—ER AND CHILD,

HO — LY IN —FANT SO TEND—ER AND MILD, SLEEP IN HEAV — EN—LY

PEACE, SLEEP IN HEAV — EN—LY PEACE.

2. Silent night, holy night! shepherds quake, at the sight
Glories stream from heaven a - far, heav'nly host sing alleluia,
Christ the Savior is born. Christ the Savior is born.

'TIS A GIFT TO BE SIMPLE

(Sing and Strum)

COME AND GO WITH ME

(Sing and Strum)

2. There will be singing in that land   3. There will be dancing in that land

GIVE ME THAT OLD TIME RELIGION

(Sing and Strum)

A		D A
2. It was good for the Hebrew children, It was good for the Hebrew children,
E7	A	A E7 A
It was good for the Hebrew children, It's good enough for me.

DOWN BY THE RIVERSIDE
(Sing and Strum)

2. I'm gonna join hands with everyone. . . .
3. I'm gonna put on my long white robe. . . .
4. I'm gonna talk with the Prince of Peace.

NOTES ON THE SIXTH STRING "E"

Three notes on the 6th string

E	F	G
(open)	1st fret	3rd fret
	1st finger	3rd finger

NUT — E
FRET 1 — F
2 — G
3

Low E   F   G

BIG E

SHORTNIN' BREAD

GOIN' DOWN THE ROAD FEELIN' BAD

LITTLE BROWN JUG

SHENANDOAH

BIG G BOOGIE

THIS TRAIN

WE WISH YOU A MERRY CHRISTMAS

3 NEW NOTES - F SHARP

A natural sign (♮) cancels a sharp sign (♯).

F# SONG

ROCKIN' GUITAR

F# IN KEY SIGNATURE MEANS ALL F's ARE SHARPED UNLESS (♮) APPEARS BEFORE THE NOTE

WHY F#
LOOK AT KEY SIGNATURE

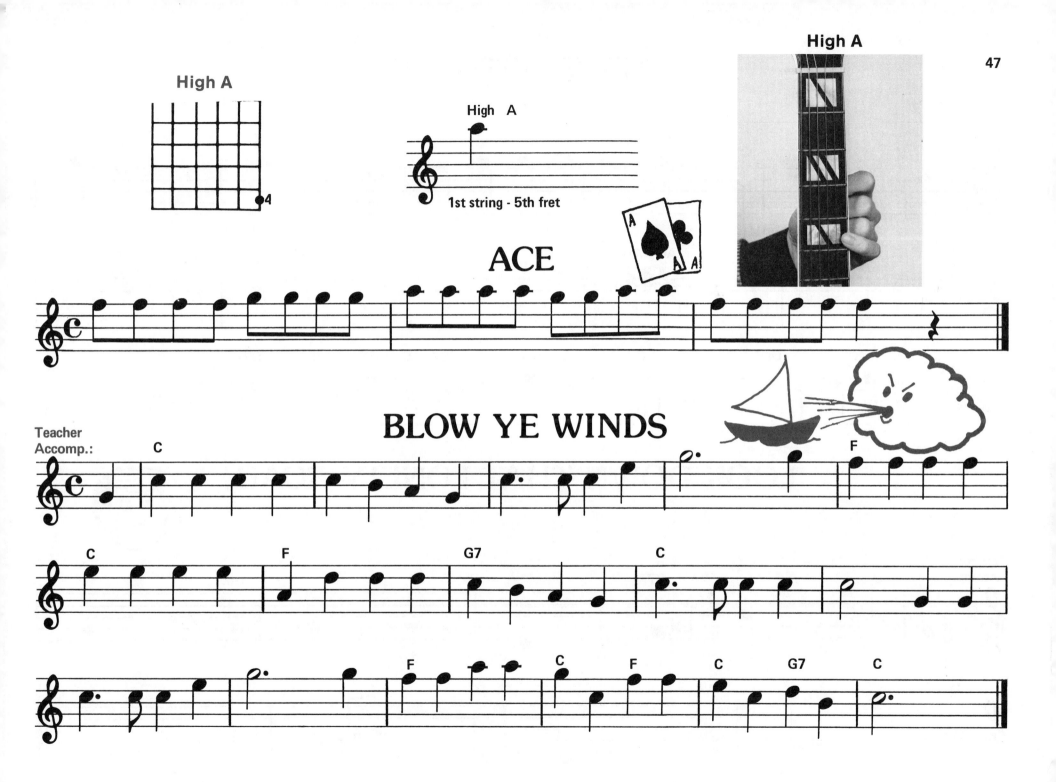

ABIDE WITH ME

LOOK DOWN THAT LONELY ROAD